MW00737732

i

ONCE UPON AN OUTHOUSE

Copyright 2000 by Nancy Millar
Published by Deadwood Publishing, Calgary, AB
Cover design and drawings by Ernie Klassen, Calgary, AB
Photographs by Judy Dahl, (JD) Claresholm, AB
Other photographs courtesy Rita MacDonald, (RM) Hanna,
and Pauline Dempsey, (PD) Calgary, and Glenbow Museum,
Calgary
Layout and interior design by Brian McCready, Calgary, AB

ISBN: 0-920109-10-1

E-mail: nemillar@telusplanet.net

Printed by Emerson Clarke Printing, Calgary
Reprinted January 2004

Other books available from Deadwood Publishing:
Remember Me As You Pass By, Stories from Alberta
Graveyards- Nancy Millar
Once Upon A Tomb, Stories from Canadian Graveyards-
Nancy Millar
Once Upon A Wedding, A Veiled History of Canada- Nancy
Millar
The Famous Five: Emily Murphy and the Case of the Missing
Persons- Nancy Millar
I Think I Should Know Those Trees, A Story of Longterm
Care- Nancy Millar

Once Upon an Outhouse

Come on in... The door's open, rest a spell! (JD)

Time out for some heavy reading

A ROSE BY ANY OTHER NAME....

It was called the outhouse, the little house, the back house and the White House.

It was called the privy, the biffy, the loo and the library.

In its grander moments, it was called the House of Lords, the Ladies' Chamber and the Throne.

In its humbler mode, it was known as the Shack Out Back, the Comfort Station, the Rest Room, the John and the You-Know-What.

In French Canadian communities in the west, it was known as the "becosse," but after a few generations that word sounded suspiciously like "backhouse."

It was called His and Hers, Men and Women, Boys and Girls and I'm Not Sure.

It had more names than any other building around the place, but it was seldom mentioned by name. Just because folks had to use it regularly didn't mean they were going to talk about it. Bodily functions weren't discussed in the early days. It was considered coarse or impolite to do so. Therefore, the seat of bodily functions wasn't talked about either...except in roundabout or humorous ways.

THE PERFECT SETTING.....

Every pioneer farmyard had to have a house, a barn and an outhouse. The house and barn were right out there where everyone could see them; the outhouse was not. If there were trees around, it was hidden among them. If there were no trees, it was sometimes attached to another outbuilding- the coal shed, wood shed or a granary. Sometimes, lacking any means of camouflage, it had to stand out like a bump on a log and so it did, but no one mentioned it. It was the invisible third party.

Ideally, the outhouse was supposed to be located downhill from the house so that sudden trips could be made more easily. It didn't matter how long it took to come back... unless you were the woman of the household. Women, it was held, used the outhouse more often than men. Better make it handy for the frail little darlings to do a little housework along the way. Thus was an outhouse path supposed to go by the garden, the wood-pile and the well, so that mother could pick vegetables on her way back, haul along a few sticks of wood and carry a pail of water- on her head presumably since she's already toting vegetables and wood.

Also, the clothesline was often strung between the little house and the big one, which meant that mama could conceivably do <u>four</u> things on her way back from the biffy. Mind you, the clothesline served another important purpose. It could be used as a guide to the outhouse during winter storms or after dark.

Multi-tasking in the good old days

FOUR ROOMS AND A PATH...

Take the story of the war bride who came to Canada in 1946. She was a city girl from Scotland, used to running water and indoor toilets. Imagine her surprise when she got to northern Alberta with her school teacher husband and discovered they had "four rooms and a path."

In other words, they had a small four-room house with a path outside that led to the toilet. Not only did she have to learn the care and feeding of an outside toilet, she also had to learn control. In the long cold winters of northern Alberta, one did not put on boots, coat, mitts and a toque to make that trip down the path unless one really had to.

It's her theory that women of her generation are made of sterner stuff when it comes to the calls of nature. "We can hold it until the cows come home," she says.

THE SEAT OF GOVERNMENT...

An outhouse wasn't a very complicated structure to build- four walls and a roof, one door and generally one or two holes on a knee-high platform. Most settlers just built one by guess and by golly, but there were plans available from farm magazines.

Once the structure was built, the back part was placed on a pit, the depth of which depended on a whole lot of things- the time of year, the energy of the digger, the type of soil. Sometimes, well organized families moved the outhouse every few years by digging a new pit right beside the old, then moving the structure and using the newly dug up dirt to cover the old pit.

One size doesn't fit all

The holes were pretty standard- small, medium and large, round or oval. Now and then would be found a square hole, a classic case of round pegs into square holes, so they weren't very common.

To accommodate different sizes, some enterprising carpenters provided an adjustable seat in the biffy. Several hole sizes were cut into one long board, the ends of which stuck out of both sides of the outhouse. You wanted a bigger hole? Just slide the board along until you found one. You wanted a heart shape? Keep looking. An oval? A triangle? They might be there.

As for ventilation, most outhouses didn't need it. There were more than enough cracks and crannies for fresh air to enter the premises, not to mention flies, wasps, spiders and every other critter that took a fancy to the place. Occasionally, a home-owner would get fancy and cut a high window into one wall or cut the traditional crescent moon shape above the outhouse door.

DEFINITION OF A PIONEER...

Anyone who had to use a biffy in winter in spite of the cold winds that took your breath away, the paths drifted with snow, the seat covered with hoar frost.

ANOTHER DEFINITION OF A PIONEER...

Anyone who had to use a biffy in summer in spite of the smells that took your breath away, the flies that owned the place and the skunks that wanted to own the place.

DOOR WARS...

Doors were a problem. First of all, there was the argument about opening in or out. Some maintained that a door should open inwards so that the person inside always had control. Others, generally the builders, preferred to have the door open outward because then it wouldn't have to fit all that exactly. If shifts happened within the structure of the outhouse, the user could compensate by pulling the door closed behind him or her and fastening it with a long wire hook or string on the inside. Generally, there was some closing arrangement on the outside of the door as well- a piece of board that swiveled on a nail or a large hook to hold the door shut. These arrangements, of course, just asked for trouble...as in the case of the kids left home alone with the hired man.

The hired man was a kid himself so when a plan was hatched by the older kids to lock one of the younger ones into the biffy, he was all for it. As soon as 10 year old Ken, the designated victim, had entered the little house and closed the door behind him, the perpetrators crept up to the door, put a sturdy board across it and quickly nailed the door shut. No matter how Ken hollered, cried and kicked the walls, they left him there until they could see the folks coming down the road. Then and only then did they release him from his privy prison. Of course, they got heck but it had been worth it, they figured. Ken has never forgiven them, and what's worse, he has never been able to exact a good revenge. In fact, he's still working on it.

Doors left another prairie kid out in the cold one windy day when she went to a neighbor's outhouse. As she sat there, an extra strong gust of wing flipped the outside latch shut. No matter how she hollered and banged, no one heard her. Through a knothole in the lumber, she could see her neighbor working away in her garden not too far away, but do you think she could make herself heard over the wind? No, not until much later when the neighbor finished thinning her radishes and realized that the girl had not been seen for awhile.

Oh Lord, make me disappear

Inevitably, people who thought they'd just leave the door open for a minute, the better to enjoy spring or the stars in the night sky, got caught. A young teacher returned home from a late night curling game and decided to leave the biffy door open for one last look at the marvelous winter scene before her. As she sat there, she thought about the marvels of nature- the heavens, the hoarfrost on the trees, a moon so bright it seemed like day- when suddenly the preacher from next door turned into his driveway. In so doing, his car lights shone directly on her, freezing her to her place like a deer caught in headlights.

From then on, she went to a different church.

ROOM WITH A VIEW...

On one of her first teaching assignments, a young
female teacher lived with an old couple on the shore of Pine
Lake in central Alberta. There was an outdoor biffy, of course.
This was before running water had come to rural areas of the
Canadian west. The biffy itself was rather nice- located in a
secluded patch of aspen overlooking the lake. The only trouble
was- there was no door. When the young teacher asked about
the possibility of adding a door, the old lady
said, "Why you wouldn't want to interfere with the view of the
lake, would you?" What could she say? So she got used to the
view of the lake- over and over again.

NEVER MIND THE VIEW...

Then there's the sad story of the old man who died while
sitting in the outhouse. Seems his son, without telling his
dad, had moved the little house onto an abandoned deep dry
hole drilled by an oil company. When granddad came out to
use the facilities that night, he was there so long the family
got worried. When they finally checked on him, he was
sitting there with a puzzled look on his face, dead as a
doornail.

The family couldn't figure it out until the grandson remembered that granddad had told him, "I always hold my breath
until I hear the plunk."

Or so the story goes.

FUR AROUND THE HOLE...

You could always tell the age of an outhouse by the pictures on the wall- if there were pictures on the wall. Many home-makers were just glad to have the thing, never mind pretty-ing it up with wallpaper and pictures and such, but some went a step further and added a few female touches.

Curtains- if there was a window; wallpaper- if there were some pieces left over from the big house; pictures cut out of magazines- if there were magazines. It was those magazine pictures that gave away the age of the place. If the styles shown in the pictures included flapper dresses and short hair, then the place was a 1920's vintage. If the Dionne Quintuplets were hanging there, it was a 1930's building, and so on.

A much admired outhouse in southern SK sported ruffled crepe paper curtains. Now that was class!

Now and then, some attention was paid to the finish of the holes. Occasionally, they were sanded around the edge, to provide a more comfortable resting place. Sometimes, they were angled to provide a better fit. And hardly ever were they lined with fur but one longtime resident of southern AB remembers seeing just such an accommodation in an out-house on a Hutterite colony. Why not? It would certainly improve the seating arrangement on cold winter nights.

As time went on, some privies sported an actual toilet seat mounted over the hole. Wishful thinking maybe?

THE INEVITABLE EATON'S CATALOGUE...

Why Eaton's is always mentioned as the toilet paper of choice in long-ago outhouses is hard to figure. There were other sources of such- Simpsons catalogue, local newspapers, the Family Herald, the Western Producer, to name just a few. There were also the tissue paper wrappers from BC peaches or Mandarin oranges. They too filled the purpose quite well. But Eaton's is top of the list. It's engraved in the folklore of outhouses.

One writer said that, by judicious use, an old catalogue should last a year. By July, you'd be down to women's underwear; by October, tools and farm supplies; by December, the index. Throughout that time, you'd also have the pleasure of looking at the catalogue items, checking out the stuff you couldn't afford. It made for a pleasant interlude, a time of daydreaming and woolgathering. Thus was the catalogue a dream machine as well as the most down-to-earth commodity around.

Then there was the time that a woman wrote to the catalogue company and ordered toilet paper. They wrote back and asked for the toilet paper page number and item number. She responded, "If I had the catalogue, I wouldn't need the toilet paper."

As catalogues got slicker and slicker- with colored pages and coated paper, they lost favour as #1 choice in the backhouse. Local newspapers and farm magazines moved out to the biffy instead.

Then toilet paper took its turn. Invented in the early 1880's complete with the perforated sections, it took awhile to catch on. Hardy folk on the prairies looked on it as somewhat sissy. Hard-up folk on the prairies looked on it as way too expensive. However, as money became more available and sissy wasn't such a sin, toilet paper became the norm.

THE HOUSE OF LORDS...

When Jean Hoare of Claresholm, AB, started her first restaurant in her ranch home, she had one bathroom only, and that one was up a flight of steep stairs. One night, a Lord Somebody-or-Other was dining at the Driftwillow Ranch and expressed a need for the bathroom. Upstairs, Jean pointed. Can't manage steps, said the Lord, I've got a bum leg. With many apologies, Jean pointed him to a disreputable old outhouse in the back yard. It was falling over, had spider webs and birds nests in it, but the Lord had to go.

Ever after, it was known at the restaurant as the House of Lords. And soon after that, Jean got another bathroom installed downstairs. The House of Lords remained for many years, however, before it finally gave up its noble title and collapsed.

Once splendid. Now abandoned. Seen better days (JD)

11

The reluctant housewife who won't go to pot

HOLDING OUT FOR A CHINOOK...

Once upon a time in the middle of a bitter winter, Mr. G. called the local doctor and asked him to come quick. "My wife is very sick," he said. "She has a terrible stomach ache. You have to come."

So the doctor came and examined Mrs. G. At the end of the examination, he diagnosed her trouble as constipation, likely brought on by a combination of winter diet (no fresh fruit or vegetables) plus a good dose of outhouse avoidance. "A classic case," he told her husband, "of waiting for a chinook." Then he made up a powdered concoction and put it into a kitchen cup. "Take a teaspoonful as soon as I leave," he told Mrs. G. "and if that doesn't bring relief, take another half teaspoonful every hour until the problem is solved."

Mr. G., a well known moonshiner, was so pleased to hear that his wife was relatively OK that he offered the doctor a taste of his new batch. "Just wait a minute," he said, "I'll get you a cupful," and he grabbed a cup from the cupboard and disappeared into his cellar. When he came back with a foaming cupful, the doctor drank it down with apparent relish before leaving for home.

About an hour later, Mr. G. was back on the phone to the doctor. "Where's that stuff you left for the Missus?" he asked. "I can't find it anywhere."

You know the end of the story. The doctor had ingested all of the constipation medicine along with the illegal booze and was out of commission for the next several days. It's not recorded what happened to Mrs. G. Maybe a chinook came along. They do that on the prairies.

DON'T TOUCH MY BIFFY...

As awful as biffies could be, they had their defenders. After all, the defenders said, biffies are quiet, they allow a little peace and quiet in busy households, they are suited to their purpose. One old gent who heard that biffies were to be abolished in his town said, "What? I have to do my business inside? It's not right."

Sid Cornish in his book, "Country Calls: Memories of a Small Town Doctor," quotes one townsperson telling him that his biffy should stay in spite of newfangled notions about indoor bathrooms. "The place has given us all a lot of relief over the years. It's like a family heirloom. It's a crying shame to tear it down," he said.

Another of Dr. Cornish's neighbors advanced the theory that outhouses should stay so that kids had something to do on Hallowe'en. If they couldn't tip over toilets, they'd do something worse, she argued. Besides, she said, they'd come in awfully handy in an emergency.

Who could argue with that?

THE THUNDER MUG...

The use of a chamber pot inside the house was discouraged, mainly because it had to be emptied outside and that was one of the nastiest jobs in a pioneer household. Only if it was very cold were the kids allowed to use one at night. Only if grandma was very sick or old could she get away with the thing. And never could the men and boys of the household use it. They already had the advantage of being able to pee outside the back door into a snow bank or bush. They couldn't have all the luck.

A chamber pot was an enamel or china container that was stored in a wash stand or under the bed. The user had to squat above or on the thing to relieve herself, then it was covered and put away until it could be emptied. They were absolutely necessary but they were at the same time a messy smelly business. And for sure, they were never discussed in polite company.

In impolite company, they were referred to as "thunder mugs" because of the noise that inevitably resulted when used. Just getting them out from under the bed caused a great clanking noise, especially in the quiet of the night- thunder #1. Then, because they were fairly tall, the pots seemed to amplify the noise associated with falling matter- thunder #2. It didn't matter how quiet, how careful, the midnight skulker was. He or she was generally found out.

The case of the disgraced chamber pot

The story is told about a store clerk who was trying to impress a lady friend. They were chatting up a storm when along came a male customer who handed him a well wrapped parcel. "My wife says this thing is much too small," he said and left the store. Without taking his eyes off the lady friend, the clerk began unwrapping the returned parcel. Without thinking, he put the contents on the counter right in front of her nose. And then, to their shared horror, they realized what it was – a chamber pot. A big fat chamber pot that hinted at private matters that would never be discussed- nor seen- by a man and woman who weren't married. Remember- these were more prudish times. The poor clerk shoved it under the counter immediately but the mood was shattered. So much for romance.

WHAT'S A GIRL TO DO...

"Going to the pot" was a secret activity. You tried to hide the noise, tried to ignore the very fact that you had to use one. People were much more prudish about such things in the early days.

Which is why a young telephone operator put the chamber pot on top of the bed to use it. The bed would muffle the sounds, she knew. She was using the landlady's pot in the landlady's bedroom but that was OK. The landlady had given her permission to use it whenever she needed to...as long as her husband wasn't home. Since husband worked on the railway, he was often away from home so the informal arrangement worked fine.

Until one day. In a hurry to get ready for work, the young woman, naked as a jaybird, tore into the bedroom across the hall and settled herself upon the pot upon the bed. Just as she got beyond the point of no-return, the bed moved, and a male voice said, "What's going on?"

What could she do? She couldn't stop. So she finished what she'd begun, put the pot back under the bed, straightened her spine and walked out of the room. How was she to know the railway had changed schedules? "I won't be home for dinner, ever, if he's at home," she told her landlady with whatever dignity was left.

In later years, she told the story with great skill and relish, but at the time she was so embarrassed and humiliated that she soon found another place to live.

BRING IN THE CHEMICALS...

Eventually, chemical toilets became available. They were knee high cans that came with an inner pail, a toilet seat, a cover and a chemical mixture that kept the smells down-almost. Generally kept out of sight in a basement or cellar or back bedroom, they were thought to be several steps above the lowly outhouse.

In the Stanmore, AB, local history book is the story of the little blue school house that boasted indoor toilets in the 1930's, the only school for miles around with such an advancedsystem. The only trouble was- they had to be emptied, and that job fell to the janitor. Every night after school, she had to remove the inner pail and lug it outside to be dumped. For that privilege, she received an extra 50 cents per month bringing her total winter salary to $5.50 a month. As welcome as any extra money was in the depression years, she was nevertheless very glad to see spring come. No more chemical toilets.

No chemicals here, horse and rider return to nature. (JD)

THE HONEY WAGON...

In 1913, the village of North Red Deer, AB, passed a bylaw outlawing outhouse pits. They were a health hazard, the new medical health officer told them, and they must be replaced by the more modern system of "honey pails." To that end, the village hired a "Scavenger" whose job it was to regularly empty the cans. They even bought a tank wagon for the job, a vehicle that was very quickly dubbed The Honey Wagon.

Not everyone loved the idea. For one thing, homeowners had to move their outhouses to the back of their lot near the lane so that the Scavenger could make his pickup. Then they had to build a flapdoor at the back of the outhouse to allow the cans in and out. What's more, the cans cost money where the old outhouse did not. And finally, they feared their municipal taxes might go up since the village had to pay the Scavenger 30 cents per pail per month.

That would add up to a nice salary for 1913...which explains how they were able to actually hire someone to do this dirty job.

A SMELLY CAPTURE...

An alleged murderer was in the firehouse cells in Olds, AB, when somehow he escaped and headed out of town. The men of the town, including the Mounties and the town police, spread out to search for the guy, one tough character, they were told.

So, the chase was on. On the outskirts of the town was a vacant lot. On the lot was an empty Honey wagon. As the searchers neared the site, out of the trapdoor on top of the Honey wagon appeared a burly form. Had to be the bad guy. He raced off past the lumberyard, the creamery, through the schoolyard and into the open fields beyond. By this time, he had half the town pursuing him and it wasn't long before the local drayman caught up with him and brought him down with a flying tackle.

Catch me, you'll be sorry

What excitement. Everyone was thrilled to have run the culprit to ground, thrilled that good had prevailed over evil, etc. Even the hero of the chase was fairly pleased. The guy wasn't all that dangerous, he said modestly, although he did admit that it was "an odorous struggle." Apparently, the Honey wagon hadn't been entirely empty.

THE DAY KATY GOT STUCK...

Every rural school had two privies- one for the boys and one for the girls. Often the door of each privy was hidden somewhat by a bit of a screen built out front. However, the interior was as plain as it could be. Two holes, toilet paper only if you were lucky, a latch that worked only if you were lucky. Girls used to go in pairs- one to hold the door shut while the other minded her business.

It really was a trial to use the bathroom, especially for girls. For one thing, they always had more underwear to deal with so the process took time. That meant that the boys could gear up to throw snowballs at the little house in the winter or rocks in the summer or insults year round. It was easier to avoid the experience entirely, which is what a lot of girls did. They were the generation that learned to hold it for a very long time!

Speaking of trials, 12 year old Katy had to go to the toilet one summer afternoon in school. The grade six teacher was reading aloud at the time, so she simply nodded when Katy asked for permission and kept on reading. Some time later, she realized that Katy had not come back.

When she looked out the window, she remembered that a sudden wind had blown up as she was reading to the students, but she had paid no attention. The story was absorbing; the students were quiet for a change. So she had read right through the storm, forgetting all about poor Katy.

Poor Katy, indeed. There she was, trapped in the outhouse which now lay on its back with the open pit in front of it. The wind had blown it over – which wasn't hard to do; most outhouses were little more than wooden boxes propped up over a pit. They had no foundation, very little support, so they were easily moved or blown over, and dear pity the person who had the bad luck to be caught there.

Katy and the flipping outhouse

That would be Katy in this case. Lying on her back, not able to push the door open above her, all she could do was holler. When finally rescue came, she still had to wait while the would-be rescuers figured out how to get her out without stepping into the open pit. Finally, they carefully rolled the little building over on its side- away from the pit- and Katy was able to crawl out. None the worse for wear, just embarrassed and a little bit mad!

For the next few days, the girls were told to use the boys' outhouse until theirs could be righted. They thought this was a big deal- they'd always wanted to know what the boys' bathroom was like. Guess what- it was just like theirs. What a disappointment.

NUMBER ONE AND NUMBER TWO...

Bodily functions were not discussed in pioneer schools; even the outhouse was not mentioned by name. Thus, children had to ask to "leave the room." In some cases, the teacher also requested that a differentiation be made between #1 and #2. Thus, when students asked to leave the room, they had to put up their hand with one finger raised or two. Then a decision would be given.

Just why the teacher cared about the exact nature of the need was never explained. Certainly she didn't have time to go along on the journey and check things out. No wonder most kids just waited until recess. If it was winter, they waited longer than that. It was just too much trouble to get to the bottom of things- for both boys and girls. Boys had a slight advantage if they had only #1 to do, but #2 required dealing with the trapdoor on the long underwear and that was just too much trouble. Easier to develop control. Women and girls didn't have a trapdoor but they also had many layers that had to be removed, unpinned, ungartered, undone. It's a wonder that anybody answered nature's call!

FIRE DRILL IN THE BIFFY...

For the first 30 years of its existence, the school in north Red Deer, AB, had plain ordinary outdoor biffies, one for the girls and one for the boys. However, in an effort to bring everything up to date in Red Deer city, the old outhouses were replaced by a much larger establishment with a boys' section, a girls' section and a saw dust burner to heat the premises. It was all quite grand, especially the heater. It seemed that they had gone about as far as they could go- but there was one problem. The sawdust burners were a fire hazard, and because the school officials could never quite bring themselves to hold a fire drill in the biffies, they were never used.

TEACHER, MAY I....

Some boys disliked school so much that they hatched a plan to undermine it, a plan that required frequent visits to the boys' outhouse. They'd take turns asking to "leave the room" and once outside, they'd pick up the shovel that was left there and they'd shovel away under the back end of the school. The idea was to dig such a deep hole that the school would tip into it, and the powers-that-be would have to cancel school indefinitely.

When the hole was finally discovered, it was- according to local legend- big enough to hold a good sized elephant. (Maybe it just seemed that big to the boys who bent their back to the task.) At any rate, it wasn't big enough to overthrow the school but it was big enough to require several days of heavy digging for some local boys.

Doing the arithmetic in pioneer schools

TRICK OR TREAT...

Toilets were an irresistible target on Hallowe'en night. Tip one over without the adults in the household catching you, and you had done something very daring indeed. Not only that but toilet-tipping was a visible sign of your mischief, and not a very serious one at that. Most households just propped the things up the next morning, grumbled a bit about stupid kids, and got on with life.

There were exceptions, however. Some adults plotted great schemes to catch the kids and prevent the inevitable. Thus did some grown men- it was mostly men- sit out in their outdoor toilets until the wee small hours on Hallowe'en night to catch the pranksters. When they did catch them and send them packing before the dirty deed was done, both sides of the equation were satisfied- the grown men because they had caught the kids, the kids because they had had a memorable scary evening. But once in awhile, the kids scored an even bigger coup. In Grande Prairie, AB, for instance, a grown man sat in wait for the midnight skulkers. They, in turn, knew he was there so they took great pains to creep up silently and with one concerted effort, push the toilet over WITH the owner in it. It's still talked about in certain circles!

In another small northern town, some of the boys threw empty cans into the hole beneath the storekeeper's biffy. She guessed the names of the culprits, marched over to the schoolhouse the next morning and turned them all in to the principal. In turn, he went with them during the noon hour and supervised their descent into the toilet hole where they had to remove the unwanted cans. Call it an education in consequences.

On another Halloween expedition, those same boys sneaked into a neighborhood biffy and painted the edge of the toilet hole with a bright sticky red paint. That wasn't nearly as much fun because they never heard if or who got caught with their pants down in the red paint. They're still wondering.

In central AB, school trustees in the Gadsby area finally got smart. Year after year on November 1, they had to come into town to set the toilets up again. Didn't matter how strong they built them each year or how much they lectured their own kids about leaving the toilets alone. Every year, the little houses went down. Finally, the trustees decided to attach them to opposite ends of the school barn, and that worked wonderfully. Tricksters on Hallowe'en didn't have time to pry out nails and remove support boards.

Not that the toilets were wonderfully built or anything. In fact, when the teacher asked that the little houses be ventilated, now that they were so close to the barn and all, one of the trustees simply took an axe to a board in the gable. That, he said, should "give the old gal enough air." It is not known if he was referring to the outhouse as a "gal" or to the teacher.

Upright now at the Sunnynook, AB, school but wait until Hallowe'en! (RM)

BANK DEPOSITS...

Ignored as a necessary evil for most of the year, outhouses came into their own at Halloween. If they weren't being tipped over, they were being painted or moved or nailed shut or booby trapped in some way. Take, eg, the Peachland, BC, outhouse that was moved from the alley behind the Bank of Montreal building on Main Street to the street in front of the bank. There, the pranksters nailed it shut and attached a sign that read, "Bank of Montreal..Large and small deposits received at all hours."

The bank manager was fit to be tied when he found it the next morning but police didn't get too excited. It was Hallowe'en, after all, and it was an outhouse, after all.

NINE AT A TIME...

This Hallowe'en story from Cochrane, AB, took two years to develop. The first year, some boys loaded the stationmaster's outdoor toilet onto an empty flatcar as it stood on the tracks in town. When the train chugged west toward Banff, bearing one lonely toilet propped up on a flat car, they figured that would be the end of the story. They also figured it was one of the best Hallowe'en tricks they'd pulled off. Toilet disappears into the sunset, nobody knows where.

But next morning, the stationmaster happened to hear a Morse code conversation between the Banff office and Calgary. We've got a toilet here, Banff told Calgary, but there's no bill of lading. Do you know anything about it?

The Cochrane agent soon figured out that it was his toilet and he had it shipped back. But he was not going to allow such foolishness another year. As a member of town council, he organized a vigilante committee of 11 men to patrol the town the next Hallowe'en. No more nonsense for this town.

Modern conveniences on the CPR?

However, the local kids heard of the plans which only made them more determined to pull off as many tricks as possible.

One back alley in town featured nine outhouses, one behind each of nine stores. They were an irresistible target so the kids organized themselves into gangs, calculated the time it would take to tip each one in turn, and still have time to run like heck and avoid the vigilantes. All went well until they tipped the toilet behind the Chinese Café. Out of the toilet came the most unholy row, hollering and beating on the walls. The noise made more noise- dogs barked, the vigilantes arrived, people came running. Turns out the recently hired Chinese cook was in the toilet as the kids tipped it, and he was not amused. In fact, he was so mad that he left the job and Cochrane shortly afterwards.

And the kids? Some caught heck, some stayed quiet, all avoided the Chinese Café for a long time.

FLASHLIGHTS FOREVER...

Outhouses ate flashlights after dark. It never failed. First you had to find the flashlight somewhere in the house- an aggravating task to begin with, then hope that it had working batteries and head out into the unknown. Once arrived at the outhouse, you had to shine the light around to make sure there were no creepy crawlies lurking in the corners, then check for spiders before settling down. But wait- where's the flashlight?

Down the hole, of course. No proper outhouse was square to the world, especially not at night when a scared kid put the flashlight on the seat- "just for a minute, dad. I didn't mean to. I'm really sorry."

Some dads got so sick of fishing the flashlight out of the murky pit that they rigged up a special wire snare to bring the goods back. Kept it handy on the outhouse wall. And for sure, they threatened that "next time, I'll hold you upside down over the hole and you can get it."

NOSING OUT THE MOONSHINE...

The trouble with moonshine liquor was its smell, an unpleasant sour fermenting smell. You could tell a mile away that something was brewing which made it tough to keep the process secret. During Prohibition days in the west, moonshine operations were set up all over the place but police often found them, either by the smell or by neighbors tattling on one another.

One moonshiner devised an elaborate system of ventilation pipes. He had both his illegal still and his toilet in his cellar. As long as he was alone, he vented the fumes from his still out through the pipes, but as soon as somebody else appeared near his house, he switched the vents to the toilet pipes. Thus did he escape detection for longer than most. Who wants to sniff out a toilet?

A proper outhouse if ever there was one! And made of brick too! (JD)

OH, TO BE IN ENGLAND...

There once was a British emigrant who missed his homeland terribly. He was glad to have land in Canada but he was still British at heart, and anything British had to be better than Canadian. To that end, he had his sister send out a weekly bundle of the London Daily Telegraph. Once he had read the familiar old papers cover to cover, he allowed them to be used in the outhouse. In fact, they were the only papers that could be used in the outhouse, British products being so much superior to Canadian. That was fine until one day, the bundle came along with a letter from Aunt Jessie who said they had measles in their British household.

Well, that put the cat among the pigeons. What if these precious papers carried the germs of measles? For once and once only, the papers were burned before they were read.

It was a long week both inside and outside the home.

WATCH OUT BELOW...

The most famous outhouse in the west belonged to the Windsor Hotel in Lundbreck, AB. The hotel built in 1905 was a two-story building- the main floor housed the bar and restaurant, the second floor housed the hotel rooms. In order to serve both floors, the owners built a two-story outhouse. From the upstairs, patrons in need could walk along a catwalk that led to their piece of the outhouse. From the downstairs, the customers simply went outside and used the bottom part of the outhouse. In order to avoid sticky situations, the two sections <u>were not</u> placed one below or above the other. They were offset with the upstairs room further back than the downstairs.

The original two story outhouse in Lundbreck, AB (Glenbow Museum)

Everything was up-to-date in Lundbreck, what's more. Instead of the old fashioned pit that was most common beneath outhouses, the Lundbreck two story had galvanized "soil pails" at the bottom of everything. It's not known how often the soil pails had to be emptied, but some poor soul must have been assigned to the job.

By the time the famous outhouse was moved to Heritage Park in Calgary, AB, in 1965, it was an outhouse for looking at, not for using. The area formerly occupied by soil pails is now used for storage, and the outhouse itself is a much admired reminder of The Way We Were.

An original one story outhouse, with other originals of farming days. (JD)

NAME THAT SEX...

One didn't talk about outhouses in polite society. They were out there, and enough said. However, now and then, someone would get original with the labels for the men's and the women's.

In Blairmore, AB, were two outhouses, one for Pointers and one for Setters.

All over the west were rooms labeled Hen and Rooster. Ewe and Ram. Jane and John. Cowgirl and Cowboy. Gals and Guys, King and Queen. Guys and Dolls.

JUST CALL IT GONE...

A farmer came out of his local bank one afternoon, scratching his head and muttering under his breath. "That damn bank," he said. "It's just like my outhouse. I deposit and I deposit, but I get nothing in return."

SPEAKING OF NAMES...

Kerry Wood in his book entitled "A Corner of Canada" wrote about the last day of the outhouses in Delburne, AB. Seems the town finally had water and sewage so the town fathers arranged an outhouse sacrifice. People brought their old biffies to main street, piled them up and with glad cries lit them on fire. Very few wept to see the old two and three holers go up in smoke and flames. In fact, most danced the night away, around and around the burning pile, the music accompanying the crackling fire.

Ever since that time, Delburne town fathers and mothers have been known as Privy Councillors.

THE CRESCENT MOON...

Years ago before most people could read, outhouses were marked with a crescent moon for women and a star or circle for men. Because men could always use the bush or a back alley, their outhouses fell into disrepair and disuse more often than women's. Thus, the outhouses that survived were marked with crescent moons until finally the symbol became a universal one.

His and hers- for better, for worse

SPEECH FROM THE THRONE...

Come to think of it, an outhouse <u>was</u> pretty funny. Everybody had to use one but nobody talked about it. Certainly, schoolkids didn't write compositions entitled, "The Historical Significance of the Outhouse" or "What I Did During my Summer Holidays in the Biffy." It was just not discussed-neither the purpose nor the building itself.

Which may be why toilet talk had to occur within the toilet itself- written or carved on the wall with pencil, pen, chalk, penknife. Some of it was mushy girl loves boy stuff. Some was more specific in nature. Sometimes, it was funny.

John Colombo's Little Book of Canadian Graffiti quotes these two passages of bathroom graffiti, both of them with tongue in cheek:

"Why go west when you can make your pile here?" (Found in a bathroom in the Maritimes.)

And this one found in an AB men's room in 1928:
> When Adam was a
> Small lad before
> Paper was invented
> He wiped his ass on
> A tuft of grass and went
> Away contented.

This was a favorite inside pay toilets:
> Here I sit all broken-hearted,
> Paid a dime but only farted.

Then there are the more modern references on bathroom walls as in:

> I think, therefore I am,
> I'm pink, therefore I'm Spam.

Or: He who stands on a toilet is high on pot.

Outhouse walls also gave the chance to leave one's name behind, as in "Betty Smith was here." That would be followed by
various smart cracks like "Why?" or "What a relief" or "I can
tell by the smell." One variation on that theme was "Betty Smith
was here, got smart and left." That line, of course, just begged
for the next line, "Left what?" And so on.

As time went along and people got more daring, the word
"Shit" began to appear regularly on outhouse walls.

> Here I sit, what a caper
> I have to shit but I'm out of paper.

Some of the "S" word nonsense was quite clever but then the
"F" word took over most of the walls. The fun changed.

PUNS IN THE OUTHOUSE...

This is a limerick that Hugh Dempsey, Editor of Alberta
History and Chief Curator Emeritus of Glenbow Museum in
Calgary remembered from his youth. Watch out for the
double meaning in the last line:

There was a young man from Clyde
Who fell down a backhouse and died,
His foolish young brother fell down another
And now they're interred(?) side by side.

ONCE UP ON A BIFFY...

In 1958, James Gladstone was named to the Canadian Senate, the first native Canadian to be so honored. He lived on the Blood Reserve in southern Alberta and this is the outhouse that served the family for years. It's got some bush around it now, but originally it stood on open prairie which meant that wind and snow could attack at will.

The Gladstone family outhouse without snow (PD)

One winter, so much snow fell and drifted that the outhouse was almost covered. Only the top 1/3 showed. Who could resist such an apportunity?

Family members tiptoed out on the drifts and had their pictures taken on the roof of the biffy. Daughter Pauline (now Mrs. Hugh Dempsey) is shown in the picture here.

The Gladstone family outhouse with snow (PD)

The drifts appear black in the picture because they are black. It's souther Alberta, remember. After the now blows in, then the dust blows in.

A BURNING HOLE...

A prairie pioneer got sick of sitting in a cold outhouse on a cold slab of wood during the winter, so he came up with a plan. He'd take spare newspapers with him to the outhouse, light them afire and drop them down the hole. After they'd burned for awhile, he'd sit himself down on a nice warm seat. That was the plan anyway.

The end didn't justify the means

One night, as usual, he lit his newspapers, threw them down the hole and sat down for some quiet contemplation. Suddenly, however, his bottom got way too hot and he realized he'd set the whole building on fire. Pulling up his pants and trying to throw snow on the fire at the same time didn't work. The outhouse and the attached chicken coop burned before his eyes.

The others in the household were not amused.

THE RETURN OF THE OUTHOUSE...

Outhouses are back in favour, not as outdoor bathrooms but as archeological digs. Turns out that people used the pit beneath their privy for all sorts of things besides the obvious- they threw old cans and bottles down there, they got rid of moonshine machinery, they lost jewelry down there.

"Privies are time capsules," is the way one enthusiastic digger describes his hobby...which means he scopes out possible sites of old privy pits during the winter months, gets any necessary permissions and then digs all summer long. As a result, he has an amazing stock of antique bottles and jars plus jewelry, machinery and various other treasures.

BUT WHAT ABOUT THE SMELL?

The present day archeological explorer doesn't have to worry about smells because the waste matter has long since turned to good rich earth. The original owners, however, were not so lucky. Some kept a bag of lime in the biffy and threw a scoopful down the hole every now and then. Others took the ashes from the woodstove and threw them down the hole. Others just kept the door open and their noses shut!

HOW MANY HOLES FOR A ROYAL VISIT...

There's more to a Royal Visit than waving and flags and sumptuous banquets. There's the matter of toilets.

When King George VI and Queen Elizabeth came to Edmonton, AB, on June 2, 1939, it was a very big deal. The city got all spruced up, civic dignitaries dug out their morning suits, wives of civic dignitaries practiced their curtsies, and ordinary people lined up for days and hours to be able to see the royal pair. It was all very exciting, but what do you do with thousands of people clamoring to be part of the event? Well, you build bleachers along the cavalcade route to begin with, and then you build toilets in the vicinity of the bleachers.

The toilets were not the portable plastic ones that appear everywhere nowadays but were proper lumber made-to-measure outhouses. They were not placed on open pits- royal noses could not be subjected to lowly smells, after all. Instead, each biffy was equipped with chemical pails.

Apparently, the toilet detail performed well. In a report written after the momentous event, the engineer in charge recorded that:
> -14 women's toilets were erected @ 8 holes each
> -15 men's toilets were erected @4 holes each and 16' of trough
> -2 small toilets were erected at the Indian Reserve
> -2 cases of toilet paper were used = 200 pkgs.

Thus, the report concluded, each hole was used on an average of 80-90 times.

WHO NEEDS A HOUSE?

Then there was the bachelor who decided he didn't need a little house in which to perform his natural bodily functions. He had the whole outdoors, after all, miles away from prying eyes on his remote homestead. So he established what might be called a parking lot behind a thicket of poplar trees, and would have lived happily ever after except that he bent over too close to a rose bush one day and tore a long rip in his precious long underwear. Now, that was a problem for two reasons: it was mighty cold that winter and he didn't know how to sew.

For awhile, he just let the underwear droop. As it crept lower and lower on his body, his feet and legs stayed fairly warm but his backside and trunk got progressively colder. That couldn't go on. Eventually, he gave in, found a long lost needle and thread and put the pieces of his underwear back to-gether again. It wasn't exactly sewing. It was more like stapling without a stapler, but it kept his nether parts warm until spring came.

Even an old outhouse is better than none. (JD)

THE ORIGINAL CRAPPER...

Thomas Crapper was a London, England, plumber who did NOT invent the flush toilet. He installed a bunch of them, however, including some for the royal family in the 1880's.

The first siphon water system was invented by another man but Crapper improved it along the way and left his name prominently displayed on the new improved version. Thus did people see time and time again the words: Crappers Improved Registered Ornamental Flush-Down Water Closet.

He also installed manhole covers all over London complete with his name emblazoned on them, but they didn't become known as Crapper Manholes. It was the water closet that first got called the crapper; then the bathroom and the purpose of the bathroom took on the name as well.

You don't like your name? Try mine.

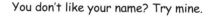

GO FIGURE...

It must be said- outhouses were not the most pleasant experience going. They were cold in winter, hot and smelly in summer, often dirty, often decrepit, a soup of germs and grime and flies.

But they are remembered by and large with forgiving pleasure. Lots of talk about the peace and quiet, the daydreaming, the privacy, the silly schoolday antics, the inevitable Hallowe'en pranks.

Could it be that outhouses represent youth, a simpler time, back to the basics, all that stuff? Or do we romanticize them because we don't have to use them anymore?

Whatever the cause, they're big right now. Outhouse collectibles of every kind are available out there-
> outhouse night-lights,
> outhouse T-shirts,
> wooden outhouse birdhouses,
> wooden outhouse-shaped toilet paper holders- of course,
> outhouse toilet seat covers with matching towels,
> outhouse hot seats that keep you from freezing your assets off,
> outhouse earrings,
> chamber pots and bedpans to serve as table centrepieces,
> quilts with an outhouse theme.

The world is crazy about outhouses, or just crazy. It's hard to tell!

In the US, outhouse races are held annually. Teams of five people enter; four push and pull the wheeled outhouse, one sits on the throne. Winners get the Crescent Moon award. What else?

So, who are we to buck the trend? Here is even more about the newly respectable and beloved outhouse! Hope you enjoy...How the West Answered the Call!

The End